PETER GOD

BY

JAMES OLIVER CURWOOD

British Library Cataloguing-in-Publication Data
A catalogue record for this book is available from the
British Library

James Oliver Curwood

James Oliver 'Jim' Curwood was an American action-adventure writer and conservationist. He was born on 12th June, 1878, in Owosso, Michigan, USA – as the youngest of four children.

He left high school before graduation, but passed the entrance exam to the University of Michigan, where he enrolled in the English department and studied journalism. After two years, he quit college to become a reporter. In 1900, Curwood sold his first story while working for the Detroit News-Tribune, and after this, his career in writing was made. By 1909 he had saved enough money to travel to the Canadian northwest, a trip that provided the inspiration for his wilderness adventure stories. The success of his novels afforded him the opportunity to return to the Yukon and Alaska for several months each year – allowing Curwood to write more than thirty such books.

By 1922, Curwood's writings had made him a very wealthy man and he fulfilled a childhood fantasy by building 'Curwood Castle' in Owosso. Constructed in the style of an eighteenth century French Chateau, the estate overlooked the Shiawassee River, and made for a truly picturesque setting. In one of the homes' two large turrets, Curwood set up his writing studio. He also owned a camp in a remote area in Baraga County, Michigan, near the Huron Mountains as well as a cabin in Roscommon, Michigan.

Curwood's adventure writing followed in the tradition of Jack London. Like London, Curwood set many of his works in the wilds of the Great Northwest and often used animals as lead characters (Kazan, Baree; Son of Kazan, The Grizzly King and Nomads of the North). Many of Curwood's adventure novels also feature romance as primary or secondary plot consideration. This approach gave his work broad commercial appeal and helped drive his appearance on several best-seller lists in the early 1920s. His most successful work was his 1920 novel, The River's End. The book sold more than 100,000 copies and was the fourth best-selling title of the year in the United States, according to Publisher's Weekly. He contributed to various literary and popular magazines throughout his career, and his bibliography includes more than 200 such articles, short stories and serializations.

Curwood was an avid hunter in his youth; however, as he grew older, he became an advocate of environmentalism and was appointed to the 'Michigan Conservation Commission' in 1926. The change in his attitude toward wildlife can be best expressed by a quote he gave in The Grizzly King: that 'The greatest thrill is not to kill but to let live.' Despite this change in attitude, Curwood did not have an ultimately fruitful relationship with nature. In 1927, while on a fishing trip in Florida, Curwood was bitten on the thigh by what was believed to have been a spider and he had an immediate allergic reaction. Health problems related to the bite escalated over the next few months as an infection set in. He died soon after in his nearby home on Williams Street, on 13th August 1927. He was aged just forty-nine, and was interred in Oak Hill Cemetery (Owosso), in a family plot.

Curwood's legacy lives on however, and his home of Curwood Castle is now a museum. During the first full weekend in June of each year, the city of Owosso holds the Curwood Festival to celebrate the city's heritage, and in addition, a mountain in L'Anse Township, Michigan was given the name Mount Curwood, and the L'Anse Township Park was renamed Curwood Park.

PETER GOD

Peter God was a trapper. He set his deadfalls and fox-baits along the edge of that long, slim finger of the Great Barren, which reaches out of the East well into the country of the Great Bear, far to the West. The door of his sapling-built cabin opened to the dark and chilling gray of the Arctic Circle; through its one window he could watch the sputter and play of the Northern Lights; and the curious hissing purr of the Aurora had grown to be a monotone in his ears.

Whence Peter God had come, and how it was that he bore the strange name by which he went, no man had asked, for curiosity belongs to the white man, and the nearest white men were up at Fort MacPherson, a hundred or so miles away.

Six or seven years ago Peter God had come to the post for the first time with his furs. He had given his name as Peter God, and the Company had not questioned it, or wondered. Stranger names than Peter's were a part of the Northland; stranger faces than his came in out of the white wilderness trails; but none was more silent, or came in and went more quickly. In the gray of the afternoon he drove in with his dogs and his furs; night would see him on his way back to the Barrens, supplies for another three months of loneliness on his sledge.

It would have been hard to judge his age—had one taken the trouble to try. Perhaps he was thirty-eight. He surely was not French. There was no Indian blood in him. His heavy beard was reddish, his long thick hair distinctly blond, and his eyes were a bluish-gray.

For seven years, season after season, the Hudson's Bay Company's clerk had written items something like the following in his record-books:

Feb. 17. Peter God came in to-day with his furs. He leaves this afternoon or to-night for his trapping grounds with fresh supplies.

The year before, in a momentary fit of curiosity, the clerk had added:

Curious why Peter God never stays in Fort MacPherson overnight.

And more curious than this was the fact that Peter God never asked for mail, and no letter ever came to Fort MacPherson for him.

The Great Barren enveloped him and his mystery. The yapping foxes knew more of him than men. They knew him for a hundred miles up and down that white finger of desolation; they knew the peril of his baits and his deadfalls; they snarled and barked their hatred and defiance at the glow of his lights on dark nights; they watched for him, sniffed for signs of him, and walked into his clever deathpits.

The foxes and Peter God! That was what this white world was made up of—foxes and Peter God. It was a world of strife between them. Peter God was killing—but the foxes were winning. Slowly but surely they were breaking him down—they and the terrible loneliness. Loneliness Peter God might have stood for many more years. But the foxes were driving him mad. More and more he had come to dread their yapping at night. That was the deadly combination— night and the yapping. In the day-time he laughed at himself for his fears; nights he sweated, and sometimes wanted to scream. What manner of man Peter God was or might have been, and of the strangeness of the life that was lived in the maddening loneliness of that mystery-cabin in the edge of the Barren, only one other man knew.

That was Philip Curtis.

. . . . .

Two thousand miles south, Philip Curtis sat at a small table in a brilliantly lighted and fashionable cafe. It was early June, and Philip had been down from the North scarcely a month, the deep tan was still in his face, and tiny wind and snow lines crinkled at the corners of his eyes. He exuded the life of the big outdoors as he sat opposite pallid-cheeked and weak-chested Barrow, the Mica King, who would have given his millions to possess the red blood in the other's veins.

Philip had made his "strike," away up on the Mackenzie. That day he had sold out to Barrow for a hundred thousand. To-night he was filled with the flush of joy and triumph.

Barrow's eyes shone with a new sort of enthusiasm as he listened to this man's story of grim and fighting determination that had led to the discovery of that mountain of mica away up on the Clearwater Bulge. He looked upon the other's strength, his bronzed face and the glory of achievement in his eyes, and a great and yearning hopelessness burned like a dull fire in his heart. He was no older than the man who sat on the other side of the table—perhaps thirty-five; yet what a vast gulf lay between them! He with his millions; the other with that flood of red blood coming and going in his body, and his wonderful fortune of a hundred thousand! Barrow leaned a little over the table, and laughed. It was the laugh of a man who had grown tired of life, in spite of his millions. Day before yesterday a famous specialist had warned him that the threads of his life were giving way, one by one. He told this to Curtis. He confessed to him, with that strange glow in his eyes,—a glow that was like making a last fight against total extinguishment,—that he would give up his millions and all he had won for the other's health and the mountain of mica.

"And if it came to a close bargain," he said, "I wouldn't hold out for the mountain. I'm ready to quit—and it's too late."

Which, after a little, brought Philip Curtis to tell so much as he knew of the story of Peter God. Philip's voice was tuned with the winds and the forests. It rose above the low and monotonous hum about them. People at the two or three adjoining tables might have heard his story, if they had listened. Within the immaculateness of his evening dress, Barrows shivered, fearing that Curtis' voice might attract undue attention to them. But other people were absorbed in themselves. Philip went on with his story, and at last, so clearly that it reached easily to the other tables, he spoke the name of Peter God.

Then came the interruption, and with that interruption a strange and sudden upheaval in the life of Philip Curtis that was to mean more to him than the discovery of the mica mountain. His eyes swept over Barrow's shoulder, and there he saw a woman. She was standing. A low, stifled cry had broken from her almost simultaneously with his first glimpse of her, and as he looked, Philip saw her lips form gaspingly the name he had spoken—Peter God!

She was so near that Barrow could have turned and touched her. Her eyes were like luminous fires as she stared at Philip. Her face was strangely pale. He could see her quiver, and catch her breath. And she was looking at him. For that one moment she had forgotten the presence of others.

Then a hand touched her arm. It was the hand of her elderly escort, in whose face were anxiety and wonder. The woman started and took her eyes from Philip. With her escort she seated herself at a table a few paces away, and for a few moments Philip could see she was fighting for composure, and that it cost her a struggle to keep her eyes from turning in his direction while she talked in a low voice to her companion.

Philip's heart was pounding like an engine. He knew that she was talking about him now, and he knew that she had cried out when he had spoken Peter God's name. He forgot Barrow as he looked at her. She was exquisite, even with that gray pallor that had come so suddenly into her cheeks. She was not young, as the age of youth is measured. Perhaps she was thirty, or thirty-two, or thirty-five. If some one had asked Philip to describe her, he would have said simply that she was glorious. Yet her entrance had caused no stir. Few had looked at her until she had uttered that sharp cry. There were a score of women under the brilliantly lighted chandeliers possessed of more spectacular beauty, Barrow had partly turned in his seat, and now, with careful breeding, he faced his companion again.

"Do you know her?" Philip asked.

Barrow shook his head.

"No." Then he added: "Did you see what made her cry out like that?"

"I believe so," said Philip, and he turned purposely so that the four people at the next table could hear him. "I think she twisted her ankle. It's an occasional penance the women make for wearing these high-heeled shoes, you know."

He looked at her again. Her form was bent toward the white-haired man who was with her. The man was staring straight over at Philip, a strange searching look in his face as he listened to what she was saying. He seemed to question Philip through the short distance that separated them. And then the woman turned her head slowly, and once more Philip met her eyes squarely—deep, dark, glowing eyes that thrilled him to the quick of his soul. He did not try to understand what he saw in them. Before he turned his glance to Barrow he saw that color had swept back into her face; her lips were parted; he knew that she was struggling to suppress a tremendous emotion.

Barrow was looking at him curiously—and Philip went on with his story of Peter God. He told it in a lower voice. Not until he had finished did he look again in the direction of the other table. The woman had changed her position slightly, so that he could not see her face. The uptilt of her hat revealed to him the warm soft glow of shining coils of brown hair. He was sure that her escort was keeping watch of his movements.

Suddenly Barrow drew his attention to a man sitting alone a dozen tables from them.

"There's DeVoe, one of the Amalgamated chiefs," he said. "He has almost finished, and I want to speak to him

11

before he leaves. Will you excuse me a minute—or will you come along and meet him?"

"I'll wait," said Philip.

Ten seconds later, the woman's white-haired escort was on his feet. He came to Philip's table, and seated himself casually in Barrow's chair, as though Philip were an old friend with whom he had come to chat for a moment.

"I beg your pardon for the imposition which I am laying upon you," he said in a low, quiet voice. "I am Colonel McCloud. The lady with me is my daughter. And you, I believe, are a gentleman. If I were not sure of that, I should not have taken advantage of your friend's temporary absence. You heard my daughter cry out a few moments ago? You observed that she was—disturbed?"

Philip nodded.

"I could not help it. I was facing her. And since then I have thought that I—unconsciously—was the cause of her perturbation. I am Philip Curtis, Colonel McCloud, from Fort MacPherson, two thousand miles north of here, on the Mackenzie Kiver. So you see, if it is a case of mistaken identity—"

"No—no—it is not that," interrupted the older man. "As we were passing your table we—my daughter—heard you speak a name. Perhaps she was mistaken. It was—Peter God."

"Yes. I know Peter God. He is a friend of mine."

12

Barrow was returning. The other saw him over Philip's shoulder, and his voice trembled with a sudden and subdued excitement as he said quickly:

"Your friend is coming' back. No one but you must know that my daughter is interested in this man—Peter God. She trusts you. She sent me to you. It is important that she should see you to-night and talk with you alone. I will wait for you outside. I will have a taxicab ready to take you to our apartments. Will you come?"

He had risen. Philip heard Barrow's footsteps behind him.

"I will come," he said.

A few minutes later Colonel McCloud and his daughter left the cafe. The half-hour after that passed with leaden slowness to Philip. The fortunate arrival of two or three friends of Barrow gave him an opportunity to excuse himself on the plea of an important engagement, and he bade the Mica King good-night. Colonel McCloud was waiting for him outside the cafe, and as they entered a taxicab, he said:

"My daughter is quite unstrung to-night, and I sent her home. She is waiting for us. Will you have a smoke, Mr. Curtis?"

With a feeling that this night had set stirring a brew of strange and unforeseen events for him, Philip sat in a softly lighted and richly furnished room and waited. The Colonel had been gone a full quarter-hour. He had left a box half filled with cigars on a table at Philip's elbow, pressing him to smoke. They were an English brand of cigar, and on the box was stamped the name of the Montreal dealer from whom they had been purchased.

"My daughter will come presently," Colonel McCloud had said.

A curious thrill shot through Philip as he heard her footsteps and the soft swish of her skirt. Involuntarily he rose to his feet as she entered the room. For fully ten seconds they stood facing each other without speaking. She was dressed in filmy gray stuff. There was lace at her throat. She had shifted the thick bright coils of her hair to the crown of her head; a splendid glory of hair, he thought. Her cheeks were flushed, and with her hands against her breast, she seemed crushing back the strange excitement that glowed in her eyes. Once he had seen a fawn's eyes that looked like hers. In them were suspense, fear—a yearning that was almost pain. Suddenly she came to him, her hands outstretched. Involuntarily, too, he took them. They were warm and soft. They thrilled him—and they clung to him.

"I am Josephine McCloud," she said. "My father has explained to you? You know—a man—who calls himself— God?"

Her fingers clung more tightly to his, and the sweetness of her hair, her breath, her eyes were very close as she waited.

"Yes, I know a man who calls himself Peter God."

"Tell me—what he is like?" she whispered. "He is tall—like you?"

"No. He is of medium height."

"And his hair? It is dark—dark like yours?"

"No. It is blond, and a little gray."

"And he is young—younger than you?"

"He is older."

"And his eyes—are dark?"

He felt rather than heard the throbbing of her heart as she waited for him to reply. There was a reason why he would never forget Peter God's eyes.

"Sometimes I thought they were blue, and sometimes gray," he said; and at that she dropped his hands with a strange little cry, and stood a step back from him, a joy which she made no effort to keep from him flaming in her face.

It was a look which sent a sudden hopelessness through Curtis—a stinging pang of jealousy. This night had set wild and tumultous emotions aflame in his breast. He had come to Josephine McCloud like one in a dream. In an hour he had placed her above all other women in the world, and in that hour the little gods of fate had brought him to his knees in the worship of a woman. The fact did not seem unreal to him. Here was the woman, and he loved her. And his heart sank like a heavily weighted thing when he saw the transfiguration of joy that came into her face when he said that Peter God's eyes were not dark, but were sometimes blue and sometimes gray.

"And this Peter God?" he said, straining to make his voice even. "What is he to you?"

His question cut her like a knife. The wild color ebbed swiftly out of her cheeks. Into her eyes swept a haunting fear which he was to see and wonder at more than once. It was as if he had done something to frighten her. "We—my father and I—are interested in him," she said. Her words cost her a visible effort. He noticed a quick throbbing in her throat, just above the filmy lace. "Mr. Curtis, won't you pardon this—this betrayal of excitement in myself? It must be unaccountable to you. Perhaps a little later you will understand. We are imposing on you by not confiding in you what this interest is, and I beg you to forgive me. But there is a reason. Will you believe me? There is a reason."

Her hands rested lightly on Philip's arm. Her eyes implored him.

"I will not ask for confidences which you are not free to give," he said gently.

He was rewarded by a soft glow of thankfulness.

"I cannot make you understand how much that means to me," she cried tremblingly. "And you will tell us about Peter God? Father—"

She turned.

Colonel McCloud had reentered the room.

With the feeling of one who was not quite sure that he was awake, Philip paused under a street lamp ten minutes after leaving the McCloud apartments, and looked at his watch. It was a quarter of two o'clock. A low whistle of surprise fell from his lips. For three hours he had been with Colonel McCloud and his daughter. It had seemed like an hour. He still felt the thrill of the warm, parting pressure of Josephine's hand; he saw the gratitude in her eyes; he heard her voice, low and tremulous, asking him to come again to-morrow evening. His brain was in a strange whirl of excitement, and he laughed—laughed with gladness which he had not felt before in all the days of his life.

He had told a great many things about Peter God that night; of the man's life in the little cabin, his loneliness, his aloofness, and the mystery of him. Philip had asked no questions of Josephine and her father, and more than once he had caught that almost tender gratitude in Josephine's eyes. And at least twice he had seen the swift, haunting fear—the first time when he told of Peter God's coming and goings at Port MacPherson, and again when he mentioned a patrol of the Royal Northwest Mounted Police that had passed Peter God's cabin while Philip was there, laid up during those weeks of darkness and storm with a fractured leg.

Philip told how tenderly Peter God nursed him, and how their acquaintance grew into brotherhood during the long gray nights when the stars gleamed like pencil-points

17

and the foxes yapped incessantly. He had seen the dewy shimmer of tears in Josephine's eyes. He had noted the tense lines in Colonel McCloud's face. But he had asked them no questions, he had made no effort to unmask the secret which they so evidently desired to keep from him.

Now, alone in the cool night, he asked himself a hundred questions, and yet with a feeling that he understood a great deal of what they had kept from him. Something had whispered to him then—and whispered to him now— that Peter God was not Peter God's right name, and that to Josephine McCloud and her father he was a brother and a son. This thought, so long as he could think it without a doubt, filled his cup of hope to overflowing. But the doubt persisted. It was like a spark that refused to go out. Who was Peter God? What was Peter God, the half-wild fox-hunter, to Josephine McCloud? Yes—he could be but that one thing! A brother. A black sheep. A wanderer. A son who had disappeared—and was now found. But if he was that, only that, why would they not tell him? The doubt sputtered up again.

Philip did not go to bed. He was anxious for the day, and the evening that was to follow. A woman had unsettled his world. His mica mountain became an unimportant reality. Barrow's greatness no longer loomed up for him. He walked until he was tired, and it was dawn when he went to his hotel. He was like a boy living in the anticipation of a great promise—restless, excited, even feverishly anxious all day. He made inquiries about Colonel James McCloud at his hotel. No one knew him, or had even heard of him. His name was not in the city directory or the telephone directory. Philip made up his mind that Josephine and her father were practically strangers in the city, and that they had come from Canada—probably Montreal, for he remembered the stamp on the box of cigars.

That night, when he saw Josephine again, he wanted to reach out his arms to her. He wanted to make her understand how completely his wonderful love possessed him, and how utterly lost he was without her. She was dressed in simple white—again with that bank of filmy lace at her throat. Her hair was done in those lustrous, shimmering coils, so bright and soft that he would have given a tenth of his mica mountain to touch them with his hands. And she was glad to see him. Her eagerness shone in her eyes, in the warm flush of her cheeks, in the joyous tremble of her voice.

That night, too, passed like a dream—a dream in paradise for Philip. For a long time they sat alone, and Josephine herself brought him the box of cigars, and urged him to smoke. They talked again about the North, about Fort MacPherson—where it was, what it was, and how one got to it through a thousand miles or so of wilderness. He told her of his own adventures, how for many years he had sought for mineral treasure and at last had found a mica mountain.

"It's close to Fort MacPherson," he explained.

"We can work it from the Mackenzie. I expect to start back some time in August."

She leaned toward him, last night's strange excitement glowing for the first time in her eyes.

"You are going back? You will see Peter God?"

In her eagerness she laid a hand on his arm.

"I am going back. It would be possible to see Peter God."

The touch of her hand did not lighten the weight that was tugging again at his heart.

"Peter God's cabin is a hundred miles from Fort MacPherson," he added. "He will be hunting foxes by the time I get there."

"You mean—it will be winter."

"Yes. It is a long journey. And"—he was looking at her closely as he spoke—"Peter God may not be there when I return. It is possible he may have gone into another part of the wilderness."

He saw her quiver as she drew back.

"He has been there—for seven—years," she said, as if speaking to herself. "He would not move—now!"

"No; I don't think he would move now."

His own voice was low, scarcely above a whisper, and she looked at him quickly and strangely, a flush in her cheeks.

It was late when he bade her good-night. Again he felt the warm thrill of her hand as it lay in his. The next afternoon he was to take her driving.

The days and weeks that followed these first meetings with Josephine McCloud were weighted with many things for Philip. Neither she nor her father enlightened him about Peter God. Several times he believed that Josephine was on the point of confiding in him, but each time there came that strange fear in her eyes, and she caught herself.

Philip did not urge. He asked no questions that might be embarrassing. He knew, after the third week had passed, that Josephine could no longer be unconscious of his love, even though the mystery of Peter God restrained him from making a declaration of it. There was not a day in the week that they did not see each other. They rode together. The three frequently dined together. And still more frequently they passed the evenings in the McCloud apartments. Philip had been correct in his guess—they were from Montreal. Beyond that fact he learned little.

As their acquaintance became closer and as Josephine saw in Philip more and more of that something which he had not spoken, a change developed in her. At first it puzzled and then alarmed him. At times she seemed almost frightened.

One evening, when his love all but trembled on his lips, she turned suddenly white.

It was the middle of July before the words came from him at last. In two or three weeks he was starting for the North. It was evening, and they were alone in the big room, with the cool breeze from the lake drifting in upon them. He made no effort to touch her as he told her of his love, but when he had done, she knew that a strong man had laid his heart and his soul at her feet.

He had never seen her whiter. Her hands were clasped tightly in her lap. There was a silence in which he did not breathe. Her answer came so low that he leaned forward to hear.

"I am sorry," she said. "It is my fault—that you love me. I knew. And yet I let you come again and again. I have done wrong. It is not fair—now—for me to tell you to go—without a chance. You—would want me if I did not love you? You would marry me if I did not love you?"

His heart pounded. He forgot everything but that he loved this woman with a love beyond his power to reason.

"I don't think that I could live without you now, Josephine," he cried in a low voice. "And I swear to make you love me. It must come. It is inconceivable that I cannot make you love me—loving you as I do."

She looked at him clearly now. She seemed suddenly to become tense and vibrant with a new and wonderful strength.

"I must be fair with you," she said. "You are a man whose love most women would be proud to possess. And yet—it is not in my power to accept that love, or give myself to you. There is another to whom you must go."

"And that is—"

"Peter God!"

It was she who leaned forward now, her eyes burning, her bosom rising and falling with the quickness of her breath.

"You must go to Peter God," she said. "You must take a letter to him—from me. And it will be for him—for Peter God—to say whether I am to be your wife. You are honorable. You will be fair with me. You will take the letter to him. And I will be fair with you. I will be your wife, I will try hard to care for you—if Peter God—says—"

Her voice broke. She covered her face, and for a moment, too stunned to speak, Philip looked at her while her slender form trembled with sobs. She had bowed her head, and for the first time he reached out and laid his hand upon the soft glory of her hair. Its touch set aflame every fiber in him. Hope swept through him, crushing his fears like a juggernaut. It would be a simple task to go to Peter God! He was tempted to take her in his arms. A moment more, and he would have caught her to him, but the weight of his hand on her head roused her, and she raised her face, and drew back. His arms were reaching out. She saw what was in his eyes.

"Not now," she said. "Not until you have gone to him. Nothing in the world will be too great a reward for you if you are fair with me, for you are taking a chance. In the end you may receive nothing. For if Peter God says that I cannot be your wife, I cannot. He must be the arbiter. On those conditions, will you go?"

"Yes, I will go," said Philip.

It was early in August when Philip reached Edmonton. From there he took the new line of rail to Athabasca Landing; it was September when he arrived at Fort McMurray and found Pierre Gravois, a half-breed, who was to accompany him by canoe up to Fort MacPherson. Before leaving this final outpost, whence the real journey into the North began, Philip sent a long letter to Josephine.

Two days after he and Pierre had started down the Mackenzie, a letter came to Fort McMurray for Philip. "Long" La Brie, a special messenger, brought it from Athabasca Landing. He was too late, and he had no instructions—and had not been paid—to go farther.

Day after day Philip continued steadily northward. He carried Josephine's letter to Peter God in his breast pocket, securely tied in a little waterproof bag. It was a thick letter, and time and again he held it in his hand, and wondered why it was that Josephine could have so much to say to the lonely fox-hunter up on the edge of the Barren.

One night, as he sat alone by their fire in the chill of September darkness, he took the letter from its sack and saw that the contents of the bulging envelope had sprung one end of the flap loose. Before he went to bed Pierre had set a pail of water on the coals. A cloud of steam was rising from it. Those two things—the steam and the loosened flap—sent a thrill through Philip. What was in the letter? What had Josephine McCloud written to Peter God?

He looked toward sleeping Pierre; the pail of water began to bubble and sing—he drew a tense breath, and rose to his feet. In thirty seconds the steam rising from the pail would free the rest of the flap. He could read the letter, and reseal it.

And then, like a shock, came the thought of the few notes Josephine had written to him. On each of them she had never failed to stamp her seal in a lavender-colored wax. He had observed that Colonel McCloud always used a seal, in bright red. On this letter to Peter God there was no seal! She trusted him. Her faith was implicit. And this was her proof of it. Under his breath he laughed, and his heart grew warm with new happiness and hope. "I have faith in you," she had said, at parting; and now, again, out of the letter her voice seemed to whisper to him, "I have faith in you."

He replaced the letter in its sack, and crawled between his blankets close to Pierre.

That night had seen the beginning of his struggle with himself. This year, autumn and winter came early in the North country. It was to be a winter of terrible cold, of deep snow, of famine and pestilence—the winter of 1910. The first oppressive gloom of it added to the fear and suspense that began to grow in Philip.

For days there was no sign of the sun. The clouds hung low. Bitter winds came out of the North, and nights these winds wailed desolately through the tops of the spruce under which they slept. And day after day and night after night the temptation came upon him more strongly to open the letter he was carrying to Peter God.

He was convinced now that the letter—and the letter alone—held his fate, and that he was acting blindly. Was this justice to himself? He wanted Josephine. He wanted her above all else in the world. Then why should he not fight for her—in his own way? And to do that he must read the letter. To know its contents would mean—Josephine. If there was nothing in it that would stand between them, he would have done no wrong, for he would still take it on to Peter God. So he argued. But if the letter jeopardized his chances of possessing her, his knowledge of what it contained would give him an opportunity to win in another way. He could even answer it himself and take back to her false word from

Peter God, for seven frost-biting years along the edge of the Barren had surely changed Peter God's handwriting. His treachery, if it could be called that, would never be discovered. And it would give him Josephine.

This was the temptation. The power that resisted it was the spirit of that big, clean, fighting North which makes men out of a beginning of flesh and bone. Ten years of that North had seeped into Philip's being. He hung on. It was November when he reached Port MacPherson, and he had not opened the letter.

Deep snows fell, and fierce blizzards shot like gunblasts from out of the Arctic. Snow and wind were not what brought the deeper gloom and fear to Fort MacPherson. La mort rouge, smallpox,—the "red death,"—was galloping through the wilderness. Rumors were first verified by facts from the Dog Eib Indians. A quarter of them were down with the scourge of the Northland. From Hudson's Bay on the east to the Great Bear on the west, the fur posts were sending out their runners, and a hundred Paul Reveres of the forests were riding swiftly behind their dogs to spread the warning. On the afternoon of the day Philip left for the cabin of Peter God, a patrol of the Royal Mounted came in on snowshoes from the South, and voluntarily went into quarantine.

Philip traveled slowly. For three days and nights the air was filled with the "Arctic dust" snow that was hard as flint and stung like shot; and it was so cold that he paused frequently and built small fires, over which he filled his lungs with hot air and smoke. He knew what it meant to have the lungs "touched"—sloughing away in the spring, blood-spitting, and certain death.

On the fourth day the temperature began to rise; the fifth it was clear, and thirty degrees warmer. His thermometer had gone to sixty below zero. It was now thirty below.

It was the morning of the sixth day when he reached the thick fringe of stunted spruce that sheltered Peter God's cabin. He was half blinded. The snow-filled blizzards cut his face until it was swollen and purple. Twenty paces from Peter God's cabin he stopped, and stared, and rubbed his eyes—and rubbed them again—as though not quite sure his vision was not playing him a trick.

A cry broke from his lips then. Over Peter God's door there was nailed a slender sapling, and at the end of that sapling there floated a tattered, windbeaten red rag. It was the signal. It was the one voice common to all the wilderness—a warning to man, woman and child, white or red, that had come down through the centuries. Peter God was down with the smallpox!

For a few moments the discovery stunned him. Then he was filled with a chill, creeping horror. Peter God was sick with the scourge. Perhaps he was dying. It might be—that he was dead. In spite of the terror of the thing ahead of him, he thought of Josephine. If Peter God was dead—

Above the low moaning of the wind in the spruce tops he cursed himself. He had thought a crime, and he clenched his mittened hands as he stared at the one window of the cabin. His eyes shifted upward. In the air was a filmy, floating gray. It was smoke coming from the chimney. Peter God was not dead.

Something kept him from shouting Peter God's name, that the trapper might come to the door. He went to the window, and looked in. For a few moments he could see nothing. And then, dimly, he made out the cot against the wall. And Peter God sat on the cot, hunched forward, his head in his hands. With a quick breath Philip turned to the door, opened it, and entered the cabin. Peter God staggered to his feet as the door opened. His eyes were wild and filled with fever.

"You—Curtis!" he cried huskily. "My God, didn't you see the flag?"

"Yes."

Philip's half-frozen features were smiling, and now he was holding out a hand from which he had drawn his mitten.

"Lucky I happened along just now, old man. You've got it, eh?"

Peter God shrank back from the other's outstretched hand.

"There's time," he cried, pointing to the door.

29

"Don't breathe this air. Get out. I'm not bad yet—but it's smallpox, Curtis!"

"I know it," said Philip, beginning to throw off his hood and coat. "I'm not afraid of it. I had a touch of it three years ago over on the Gray Buzzard, so I guess I'm immune. Besides, I've come two thousand miles to see you, Peter God—two thousand miles to bring you a letter from Josephine McCloud."

For ten seconds Peter God stood tense and motionless. Then he swayed forward.

"A letter—for Peter God—from Josephine McCloud?" he gasped, and held out his hands.

An hour later they sat facing each other—Peter God and Curtis. The beginning of the scourge betrayed itself in the red flush of Peter God's face, and the fever in his eyes. But he was calm. For many minutes he had spoken in a quiet, even voice, and Philip Curtis sat with scarcely a breath and a heart that at times had risen in his throat to choke him. In his hand Peter God held the pages of the letter he had read.

Now he went on:

"So I'm going to tell it all to you, Curtis—because I know that you are a man. Josephine has left nothing out. She has told me of your love, and of the reward she has promised you—if Peter God sends back a certain word. She says frankly that she does not love you, but that she honors you above all men—except her father, and one other. That other, Curtis, is myself. Years ago the woman you love—was my wife."

Peter God put a hand to his head, as if to cool the fire that was beginning to burn him up.

"Her name wasn't Mrs. Peter God," he went on, and a smile fought grimly on his lips. "That's the one thing I won't tell you, Curtis—my name. The story itself will be enough.

"Perhaps there were two other people in the world happier than we. I doubt it. I got into politics. I made an enemy, a deadly enemy. He was a blackmailer, a thief, the head of a political ring that lived on graft. Through my efforts he was exposed, And then he laid for me—and he got me.

"I must give him credit for doing it cleverly and completely. He set a trap for me, and a woman helped him. I won't go into details. The trap sprung, and it caught me. Even Josephine could not be made to believe in my innocence; so cleverly was the trap set that my best friends among the newspapers could find no excuse for me.

"I have never blamed Josephine for what she did after that. To all the world, and most of all to her, I was caught red-handed. I knew that she loved me even as she was divorcing me. On the day the divorce was given to her, my brain went bad. The world turned red, and then black, and then red again. And I—"

Peter God paused again, with a hand to his head.

"You came up here," said Philip, in a low voice.

"Not—until I had seen the man who ruined me," replied Peter God quietly. "We were alone in his office. I gave him a fair chance to redeem himself—to confess what he had done. He laughed at me, exulted over my fall, taunted me. And so—I killed him."

He rose from his chair and stood swaying. He was not excited.

"In his office, with his dead body at my feet, I wrote a note to Josephine," he finished. "I told her what I had done, and again I swore my innocence. I wrote her that some day she might hear from me, but not under my right name, as the law would always be watching for me. It was ironic that on that human cobra's desk there lay an open Bible, open at the Book of Peter, and involuntarily I wrote the words to Josephine—PETER GOD. She has kept my secret, while the law has hunted for me. And this—"

He held the pages of the letter out to Philip.

"Take the letter—go outside—and read what she has written," he said. "Come back in half an hour. I want to think."

Back of the cabin, where Peter God had piled his winter's fuel, Philip read the letter; and at times the soul within him seemed smothered, and at times it quivered with a strange and joyous emotion.

32

At last vindication had come for Peter God, and before he had read a page of the letter Philip understood why it was that Josephine had sent him with it into the North. For nearly seven years she had known of Peter God's innocence of the thing for which she had divorced him. The woman— the dead man's accomplice—had told her the whole story, as Peter God a few minutes before had told it to Curtis; and during those seven years she had traveled the world seeking for him—the man who bore the name of Peter God.

Each night she had prayed God that the next day she might find him, and now that her prayer had been answered, she begged that she might come to him, and share with him for all time a life away from the world they knew.

The woman breathed like life in the pages Philip read; yet with that wonderful message to Peter God she pilloried herself for those red and insane hours in which she had lost faith in him. She had no excuse for herself, except her great love; she crucified herself, even as she held out her arms to him across that thousand miles of desolation. Frankly she had written of the great price she was offering for this one chance of life and happiness. She told of Philip's love, and of the reward she had offered him should Peter God find that in his heart love had died for her. Which should it be?

Twice Philip read that wonderful message he had brought into the North, and he envied Peter God the outlaw.

The thirty minutes were gone when he entered the cabin. Peter God was waiting for him. He motioned him to a seat close to him.

"You have read it?" he asked.

Philip nodded. In these moments he did not trust himself to speak. Peter God understood. The flush was deeper in his face; his eyes burned brighter with the fever; but of the two he was the calmer, and his voice was steady.

"I haven't much time, Curtis," he said, and he smiled faintly as he folded the pages of the letter, "My head is cracking. But I've thought it all out, and you've got to go back to her—and tell her that Peter God is dead."

A gasp broke from Philip's lips. It was his only answer.

"It's—best," continued Peter God, and he spoke more slowly, but firmly. "I love her, Curtis. God knows that it's been only my dreams of her that have kept me alive all these years. She wants to come to me, but it's impossible. I'm an outlaw. The law won't excuse my killing of the cobra. We'd have to hide. All our lives we'd have to hide. And—some day—they might get me. There's just one thing to do. Go back to her. Tell her Peter God is dead. And—make her happy—if you can."

For the first time something rose and overwhelmed the love in Philip's breast.

"She wants to come to you," he cried, and he leaned toward Peter God, white-faced, clenching his hands. "She wants to come!" he repeated. "And the law won't find you. It's been seven years—and God knows no word will ever go from me. It won't find you. And if it should, you can fight it together, you and Josephine."

Peter God held out his hands.

"Now I know I need have no fear in sending you back," he said huskily. "You're a man. And you've got to go. She can't come to me, Curtis. It would kill her—this life. Think of a winter here—madness—the yapping of the foxes—"

He put a hand to his head, and swayed.

"You've got to go. Tell her Peter God is dead—"

Philip sprang forward as Peter God crumpled down on his bunk.

After that came the long dark hours of fever and delirium. They crawled along into days, and day and night Philip fought to keep life in the body of the man who had given the world to him, for as the fight continued he began more and more to accept Josephine as his own. He had come fairly. He had kept his pledge. And Peter God had spoken.

"You must go. You must tell her Peter God is dead."

And Philip began to accept this, not altogether as his joy, but as his duty. He could not argue with Peter God when he rose from his sick bed. He would go back to Josephine.

For many days he and Peter God fought with the "red death" in the little cabin. It was a fight which he could never forget. One afternoon—to strengthen himself for the terrible night that was coming—he walked several miles back into the stunted spruce on his snowshoes. It was mid-afternoon when he returned with a haunch of caribou meat on his shoulder. Three hundred yards from the cabin something stopped him like a shot. He listened. From ahead of him came the whining and snarling of dogs, the crack of a whip, a shout which he could not understand. He dropped his burden of meat and sped on. At the southward edge of a level open he stopped again. Straight ahead of him was the cabin. A hundred yards to the right of him was a dog team and a driver. Between the team and the cabin a hooded and coated figure was running in the direction of the danger signal on the sapling pole.

With a cry of warning Philip darted in pursuit. He overtook the figure at the cabin door. His hand caught it by the arm. It turned—and he stared into the white, terror-stricken face of Josephine McCloud!

"Good God!" he cried, and that was all.

She gripped him with both hands. He had never heard her voice as it was now. She answered the amazement and horror in his face.

"I sent you a letter," she cried pantingly, "and it didn't overtake you. As soon as you were gone, I knew that I must come—that I must follow—that I must speak with my own lips what I had written. I tried to catch you. But you traveled faster. Will you forgive me—you will forgive me—"

She turned to the door. He held her.

"It is the smallpox," he said, and his voice was dead.

"I know," she panted. "The man over there—told me what the little flag means. And I'm glad—glad I came in time to go in to him—as he is. And you—you—must forgive!"

She snatched herself free from his grasp. The door opened. It closed behind her. A moment later he heard through the sapling door a strange cry—a woman's cry—a man's cry—and he turned and walked heavily back into the spruce forest.